LIZARDS IN THE LUNCH LINE

Want more books by Debbie Dadey?

Swamp Monster in Third Grade

The Slime Wars

Coming soon . . .

Slime Time!

And don't forget to check out . . .

The Adventures of
THE
BAILEY SCHOOL KIDS®

Ghostville Elementary®

BY DEBBIE DADEY AND MARCIA THORNTON JONES

LIZARDS IN THE LUNCH LINE

BY DEBBIE DADEY
ILLUSTRATIONS BY MARGEAUX LUCAS

A
LITTLE APPLE
PAPERBACK

SCHOLASTIC
NEW YORK   TORONTO   LONDON   AUCKLAND   SYDNEY
MEXICO CITY   NEW DELHI   HONG KONG   BUENOS AIRES

To my favorite little monsters —
Nathan, Becky, and Alex Dadey,
with special thanks to my
wonderful editor, Maria Barbo

ISBN 0-439-63161-0

Text copyright © 2004 by Debra S. Dadey.
Illustrations copyright © 2004 by Scholastic Inc.
SCHOLASTIC, LITTLE APPLE, and associated logos are trademarks and/or registered
trademarks of Scholastic Inc.

12 11 10 9 8 7 6 5 4   4 5 6 7 8 9/0

Printed in the U.S.A.   40
First printing, March 2004

CONTENTS

1

Dominick

"You're lying," Dominick told Jake. The two cousins sat on a big rock deep inside a swamp. Dominick's hair stuck up in one long fin in the middle of his head and Jake's stood up in green points, but that wasn't the only difference between the two swamp monsters. Even though Dominick was the same age as Jake, he towered over his smaller cousin.

Jake's face turned from green to red. He clenched his fists and splashed swamp water with his spiked tail. "I'm not lying," he shouted. "I really did spend the night in a webless creature's house and I really did go to one of their schools."

"Yeah, sure you did," Dominick said as he rolled his eyes. "And I ate dinner with King Neptune last night."

"Nancy will tell you the truth," Jake said, pointing to where his younger sister was playing mud ball with some friends in the swamp water. "She saw me there."

Jake put his webbed hands up to his mouth and yelled, "Nancy, come here and tell Dominick the truth."

Nancy swam over and pulled her green body up onto the rock. She flung back her stringy blond hair and asked, "What are you guys talking about?"

"Jake's been lying to me about living with webless creatures," Dominick said. "He said he ate these things called cheeseburgers that tasted better than crawfish."

Nancy shrugged. "It's true," she said matter-of-factly. "Jake really was taken off by four webless creatures and even spent the night inside one of their houses."

Jake nodded. "That was Tommy. He has these really strange white things you lay your head on to sleep. They're softer than swamp mud, but they're really dry."

"I didn't know if I'd ever see Jake again," Nancy admitted. "I thought he might stay webless forever. He looked so weird without scales. It wasn't natural."

Dominick rolled his green eyes and snorted in disbelief.

"I got in *big* trouble for being gone from home for so long," Jake said. "This is the first time I've been allowed out of Mom's sight in two weeks."

Dominick slumped back onto the moss-covered rock and flicked a piece of swamp-

weed off his bare green chest. "You're making this all up," he said. "Webless creatures aren't real. My dad told me so. And there is NO WAY you turned into one."

Nancy pushed her messy hair out of her eyes and frowned at her cousin. "You're the one who told us that your friend got put in a webless creature's zoo."

Now it was time for Dominick to turn red. "I made that all up," he said softly.

Nancy roared her loudest swamp monster yell. The waters of the swamp shivered as she poked Dominick in the stomach. "You mean, you lied to us?" she fumed.

Dominick snarled back. "Just like you're lying to me now."

"I don't have to listen to this," Nancy snapped and dived headfirst into the murky swamp water.

"We're not lying," Jake said.

"Prove it," Dominick told him.

Jake thought for a moment. "Okay, come on," he said. "Follow me."

2

Webless Creatures

Jake swam fast, but Dominick kept up with him. After about ten minutes Jake poked the green points of his hair up out of the swamp water. Dominick popped his head up beside Jake. The two swamp creatures were hidden among the weeds and scraggly trees of the swamp.

"Are you sure this is safe?" Dominick whispered. "My dad told me to never go beyond the big mangrove tree." Dominick nodded toward the big tree that cast shadows over this side of the swamp. The tree's long limbs hung out over the water, but the two boys were way past the big mangrove.

Jake shrugged. "It's okay as long as we're careful. Just don't tell Nancy. I don't want to get grounded again."

"I won't say anything," Dominick told him. "I don't want to get in trouble with my dad."

"That's them," Jake whispered, pointing toward a group of four human kids.

"Wow!" Dominick breathed in admiration.

Jake could tell that it was the first time Dominick had ever seen webless creatures. Jake couldn't help boasting a little bit. "I know them. Emily is the girl. Tommy is the one with the yellow hair. They're my friends."

"Great balls of mud!" Dominick exclaimed. "What are they doing?"

Jake watched two of the webless boys toss a white ball back and forth. "That's

Ryan and Frank. They're playing baseball. I saw it on Tommy's TV."

Dominick had this weird look on his face. So Jake explained about TV. "It's this box that little bitty people are in. The little people play games and eat all kinds of neat-looking food. They even put dirty clothes in white boxes and the clothes come out clean."

Dominick nodded like this made perfect sense to him. "Let's go talk to them," Dominick suggested.

Jake shook his pointed head. "I'm not sure if that's such a good idea. It's dangerous. What if some grown-up webless creatures are around? There's no telling what they might do to us."

"Come on," Dominick begged. "I just want to see what the webless creatures are like. You said they were your friends. Prove it. Besides, I don't see anyone else around."

Jake hesitated. He knew what it was like to be fascinated by the webless creatures. Before he'd met them, Jake had always wondered about them. He'd found out they were really great, at least most of them. It would be nice to talk to his webless friends again. But he knew it was dangerous.

"No," he told Dominick. "I almost died the last time I was on dry land. Being out of the water too long isn't safe for a swamp monster."

"It'll just be for a second," Dominick insisted. "What could happen?"

Jake didn't want to think about what horrible things could happen. A picture of being caught in a net and taken to a laboratory for investigation flashed through his mind. He shook his head. "No, it's not worth it."

But Dominick wasn't going to take no

for an answer. He stomped out of the
swamp before Jake could grab him. Muddy
water dripped off Dominick's green body
and swampweed hung from his arms. The
four kids took one look at Dominick and
screamed.

3

Green Goose Bumps

Jake had no choice. He jumped out of the swamp to help Dominick. The cool late afternoon air gave Jake's scaly skin goose bumps, but Jake couldn't worry about that. He had to help Dominick.

When Emily saw Jake, she stopped screaming. "Jake, is that really you?" she asked.

Jake grinned. Emily had remembered him. "Hi," he said. "This is my cousin Dominick. He wanted to see if you guys were real."

"Hi," Dominick said with a big wave of his webbed hand. "Awesome to meet you."

"Nice to meet you, too," Emily said with a gulp.

The skinny boy named Ryan stood there with his mouth open. The sun flashed off Ryan's braces. But the tall kid named Frank shook his head. "I see it, but I don't believe it," he said. "You look like Jake, only green."

Tommy laughed. "I told you guys that Emily and I saw Jake as a swamp monster. Now you know we were telling the truth."

Frank couldn't help himself. He poked a finger at the webbing on Jake's hand. "It's not a costume," Frank said with a gulp.

"I told you swamp monsters were real," Emily told Frank and Ryan. "There are whole families of swamp monsters living in that swamp."

Ryan looked at the swamp and his face turned a little green. "Nothing personal, Jake, but that's kind of creepy."

Jake smiled. "Don't worry. It's scary for us that there are so many webless creatures like you around."

Ryan nodded. "Good point," he said. Ryan stood very still while Dominick poked his cheeks and sniffed his hair.

Dominick walked around all the kids and touched their clothes. He was particularly amazed with Frank's new sneakers. "Jake, these things on the end of his legs light up!"

"They're called shoes," Frank explained. Dominick nodded his head in fascination.

"Jake," Emily said, trying to ignore Dominick's webbed fingers as they ran through her hair. "It's great to see you, but isn't it dangerous for swamp monsters to be out in the open like this? This is a public park. Anyone can use it."

Jake looked around nervously. The little clearing by the swamp looked deserted. He

was worried that another webless creature might come along. He knew he could trust these four humans, but anyone else would probably put him and his cousin in the zoo. "You're right, Emily," Jake said. "We'd better get going. Come on, Dominick."

Dominick didn't budge. He was trying to toss Ryan's ball up in the air and catch it. His slippery webbed hands made it hard. Dominick did manage to throw it up in the air, but it bonged him on the nose and he let out a loud swamp monster yelp.

"Come on, Dominick," Jake said, grabbing his cousin's elbow. "We'd better get back in the swamp."

Dominick dug his webbed toes into the ground and shook his head. "I'm not going anywhere. This is cool. I'm staying right here to find out more about life on land."

Jake gulped. Dominick was much bigger than him, and if he didn't want to go, Jake couldn't force him. "Coming out here was a big mistake," Jake said. "We've got to get back in the swamp before it's too late."

Emily gasped. "Oh my gosh, it *is* too late. Someone's coming!"

4

Creepy

"Hurry," Tommy said. "Hide behind these trees."

The four kids and two swamp monsters squeezed behind a clump of trees as two teenagers walked into the clearing. "This place is creepy," the teenage girl squealed. "I bet there are all kinds of wild creatures around here."

The boy laughed and said, "Don't be silly. The only thing in that stinking swamp is dead bugs."

Dominick snorted, but Jake put his hand over Dominick's mouth before he could say anything. Jake's mouth went dry when he

saw the two teenagers spread out a picnic
lunch. They didn't look like they were going
to leave anytime soon. The worst part was
that the teenagers sat between the kids and
the swamp. There was no way Jake and
Dominick could get back into the mucky

waters without the teenagers seeing them. Emily motioned for them to follow her.

"Where are we going?" Dominick asked.

"We've got to get you out of here," she said. "We can go to my house."

Jake hesitated. He didn't want to get too far from the swamp. "It's okay," Tommy said. "If you need water, we could turn the hose on you."

Jake didn't know what a hose was, but he trusted Tommy and Emily. He had to.

Luckily, Emily's house wasn't too far away, and the two swamp monsters were able to stay in the cover of the trees almost the whole way. "Whew!" Emily said after she had led them into her kitchen and shut the door.

"What about your parents?" Frank asked.

Emily sat down at the kitchen table. "It's

all right," she said. "My mom won't be home from the store for at least another hour and Dad is working today. My sister is at soccer practice until dinnertime."

"Thanks for letting us hide here," Jake said. "We'll only stay for a few minutes." He sat at the table beside Emily. His skin felt really funny. He wondered how long it was safe to be out of the swamp. Dominick didn't seem to feel strange at all. In fact, he couldn't take his eyes off the things in Emily's kitchen.

"What's this?" he asked, poking his webbed finger at a black box. Dominick jumped backward as the lights flashed inside the microwave.

"That's how we cook our food," Emily explained as she hopped up to turn the microwave oven off.

"Cook?" Jake asked.

Emily nodded. "Sure, that's when we heat up our food so we can eat it without getting sick."

That sounded pretty strange to Jake. Everything he ate was swamp temperature. But Dominick was already checking out something else. "What's this?" Dominick pushed a button on the front of the refrigerator. Ice shot out at his green skin.

"Ahhhhh!" he screamed. "It's killing me!"

Ryan laughed. "It's just ice. It's how we make our drinks cold."

Dominick shook his head. "You want your drinks cold and your food hot? What's wrong with just regular temperature?"

"He does have a point there," Frank agreed as he picked up the ice off the floor. Unfortunately, Frank missed a piece and Dominick stepped on it.

"Ye-owwww!" Dominick screamed as he

slid across the floor on his tail and landed with a thump against the kitchen door.

"Are you all right?" Emily asked. She helped Dominick up into a chair.

Dominick rubbed his head and moaned. "This place is dangerous."

"Sorry about that," Emily said. "How about a snack?" Emily opened the refrigerator and pulled out grapes, apples, and sodas. Frank helped her by grabbing cheese and carrots.

"No!" Jake screamed, but it was too late.

5

Carrots

"Stop!" Emily screamed when she realized her mistake.

But it was too late. Dominick had already taken a big bite of a bright orange carrot. "What's wrong?" Dominick asked, with chunks of carrots dribbling out of his mouth.

"Spit it out," Jake yelled.

Dominick shook his head and stuffed another carrot into his mouth. "No, it tastes great," he mumbled.

"You don't understand," Jake said. "That's what made me turn into a human."

"Carrots?" Ryan asked.

"Uh-oh," Frank said. "I didn't know that. Why didn't you ever tell me?"

"Let's get it out of his mouth," Jake yelled. The kids grabbed Dominick's slippery arm to get the carrots. But it was too late.

Dominick fell to the floor and howled in pain, "Help, my head is killing me!" All the faces around him swirled together into one huge face and he felt like throwing up.

Dominick reached out to Jake and begged, "Help me!" Dominick grabbed the fin in the middle of his head. He closed his eyes and fainted.

"Did I kill him?" Frank moaned. All the kids stood around as Dominick lay still on the floor.

Jake knelt down next to his cousin and felt his neck. "I think he's okay; he's just really sick. Carrots make me sick, too."

Emily jumped back from Dominick. "He's changing!"

The kids stared as Dominick's skin slowly changed from bright green to a pale yellow. "This is so cool," Ryan said.

"Look at his feet!" Tommy said. Dominick's huge webbed feet shrank until the webs were gone and only very white human feet remained.

Ryan clutched his stomach as he stared at Dominick. "I think I'm going to be sick," Ryan groaned.

"That's the strangest thing I've ever seen," Frank said, staggering back against the kitchen counter. "It's like a video game come to life."

"That's no game," Jake said sadly, "that's my cousin. I just don't know what I'm going to do about it."

Dominick shook his head and sat up.

"Wow," he said. "Those carrots have quite a kick." He rubbed his head with his webless hand.

Dominick suddenly noticed his white skin and webless hands. "This is awesome!" he shouted. He stood up and danced around on his new feet. "It's just like you said, Jake. I'm a webless creature."

Dominick grabbed a carrot and thrust it at Jake. "You eat one, too. Then we can go to school and I'll know what it's really like to be one of the webless creatures."

Jake looked at Emily. She frowned. He knew what she was thinking. Two swamp monsters in one school might be two swamp monsters too many.

6
School

"I can't believe you did it," Emily told Jake the next morning at school. They were standing in the hallway. Dominick and Tommy had already gone into the classroom. Ryan and Frank were in another third-grade class.

Jake shrugged and scratched his nowwhite arm. "I couldn't leave Dominick. I have to keep an eye on him. He's a little . . . high-strung."

Emily rolled her eyes. "That's the truth. He used my toothpaste to draw on the bathroom wall."

31

"That's not as bad as what he did last night at Tommy's house," Jake said.

"What did Dominick do?" Emily asked.

Jake leaned close to Emily and whispered, "You know that fish tank Tommy has in his family room?"

Emily nodded. "They have some really neat exotic fish in there."

Jake shook his head. "Not anymore, they don't. Dominick had a midnight snack."

Emily put her hand over her mouth to stifle a squeal. She couldn't help but giggle. "It's a good thing my teacher, Mrs. Varga, doesn't have any fish."

The two kids went into the classroom and found Tommy on his knees picking up little scraps of paper. He rolled his eyes and said, "That Dominick is starting to bug me. Look at this mess he made."

Every classroom in Glenstone Elementary had its own sink. Dominick stood by the sink in the back of the room, splashing water all over himself. A puddle of water formed around his feet, and his clothes were dripping water. Luckily, Mrs. Varga wasn't in the room yet.

"What are you doing?" Emily hissed, trying not to let all the other kids in the classroom hear her.

Dominick shrugged. "I just needed to get wet. I don't know how you webless creatures stand being dry all the time. It's so itchy and uncomfortable."

Jake had to agree. Sure, it was exciting to be a human. And he definitely liked seeing Emily and Tommy again, but his skin felt really strange.

"Maybe that's because it's hot outside

today," Emily explained. "We only have a few weeks left until summer vacation!"

"Hey, it's Mr. Smarty-Pants."

Jake snapped his head around. He recognized that voice.

The classroom bully, Ted, pushed up against Jake. "Where's your Halloween costume today?" Ted asked.

Jake gulped. The last time he'd been a human, Ted had seen him change back into a swamp monster.

Ted had screamed even though Jake had fibbed that he was wearing a costume.

"What are you doing back here, anyway?" Ted asked, getting closer to Jake and frowning.

Emily pulled on Ted's arm. "Leave him alone," she said. "Jake's family might move here."

"He'd better not," Ted muttered. "I don't like . . ." But that's as far as he got because just then, a huge splash of water got him right in the face. Ted whirled around to face Dominick, ready to fight.

7

Crazy

"Where'd you come from?" Ted asked Dominick. "Is this bring-a-geek-to-school month?"

"Dominick is my cousin," Jake said quickly.

"Yeah," Emily said to Ted. "Just leave them alone."

"Come on, guys," Tommy added. "Let's go sit down before Mrs. Varga gets here."

Dominick didn't listen to Tommy. He had other things on his mind, like the white bottles on the counter. He grabbed one of them and pulled the top off. "Yum," he said.

Ted and Emily stared in amazement as

Dominick gulped down one bottle of glue and grabbed another. Ted laughed. "You're crazy. I like that."

Dominick licked his sticky lips. "This stuff is good."

Emily snatched the bottle away. "This isn't a milk shake, you know. It can't be good for you."

"All right, students," Mrs. Varga said as she came into the room with a piece of pink paper in her hand. "Let's take our seats and welcome Jake and his cousin Dominick to our class."

Jake sat down next to Emily while Dominick sat down next to Ted. As soon as all the other kids in the class were in their seats, Mrs. Varga started a spelling lesson.

Jake listened carefully and quickly memorized every word that Mrs. Varga wrote on the board. Swamp monsters have incredible memories, which is helpful not only for remembering their way around the swamp but also for memorizing human spelling lists.

Dominick was concentrating on something, too, but it wasn't Mrs. Varga. He couldn't take his eyes off Ted.

Ted was having pencil races on his desk, and he loved having an audience. He rolled two pencils to see which one was faster. Then he poked the girl in front of him with his eraser until she jumped.

Ted grinned at Dominick before whispering, "Watch this." Ted folded his work sheets into paper airplanes. Whenever Mrs. Varga wrote on the board, Ted tossed an airplane. One flew into Emily's back and another zipped by the teacher's desk. By the time Mrs. Varga turned around, the planes had already landed. She didn't see them,

but she did hear the snickers of some of the students.

"What's going on?" Mrs. Varga asked. "Ted?"

Ted sat up straight and looked innocent. "Yes, Mrs. Varga?"

"Are you up to mischief?" she asked. She knew from experience that if anyone was up to no good, it was probably Ted.

Ted put his hand over his heart and acted likc hc was in pain. "Why, Mrs. Varga. How could you even think such a thing? I'm hurt."

Mrs. Varga shook her head and sat down at her desk. Ted winked at Dominick.

Jake stared in horror as Dominick winked back.

8

Food Fight

Jake grabbed Dominick's arm on the way to music class. "We have to get back to the swamp," Jake whispered to his cousin. "We could turn back into swamp monsters any second now."

Dominick grinned at Jake with orange teeth. "Not me," Dominick said. "I'm not stupid. I figured this carrot thing was only temporary, so I brought extras." Dominick held up a huge brown paper bag filled with the carrots from Emily's refrigerator.

Jake's mouth hung open in shock and Dominick stuck a carrot in it. "You'd better eat one of these," Dominick said. "I'm not going anywhere yet."

"But what about our parents?" Jake asked. He knew the two weeks he had been grounded after the first time he became human would be a swamp pebble compared to how much trouble he was going to be in this time. His parents would never believe that he had turned into a human to keep Dominick out of trouble.

Even *that* plan didn't seem to be working very well. Dominick ignored Jake's concern and rushed into music class with Ted. The two boys had their heads together in the front row when Jake sat down beside Frank.

"How's Dominick doing?" Frank asked.

Jake rolled his eyes and groaned, "Not good."

Jake knew that Dominick and Ted together could only mean trouble, and Jake was right.

When Miss Pratt blew on her recorder to start class, bubbles came out of the end. Every kid in class laughed, but no one laughed as hard as Dominick and Ted.

Later that day in the cafeteria line, Dominick and Ted were about five people ahead of Jake and his friends. Emily shook her head when she saw Ted fill his tray with a huge mound of peas. "That can't be good," Emily said.

Jake thought the peas looked okay so he took a big scoop, too, but he almost dropped his food when he spotted Dominick's neck. Gills were forming and his cousin didn't  seem to notice. Dominick spooned an enormous pile of mashed potatoes onto his tray while Jake tried to get his attention. "Psst, Dominick!" Jake hissed.

Dominick didn't even turn around. He was busy pouring green relish onto his potatoes. Jake grabbed Emily's arm. "We have to get Dominick out of here before he turns back into a swamp monster!" Jake said. He grabbed a carrot from the lunch line. He had a horrible feeling that Dominick would morph into a monster right in front of everyone. What if they both changed at the same time?

Frank snorted. "Our school could be famous. We'd be on TV for having a lizard in the lunch line!"

Tommy laughed, but Ryan asked, "Do you really think Dominick will change here?" Jake shrugged and shuddered at the thought.

"It's all right," Emily said as the kids carried their trays to a table. "He's chewing a carrot now."

"I hope he doesn't pass out," Jake said. Emily, Jake, Tommy, and Ryan watched Dominick. He sat beside Ted at the next table. Dominick did put his head down for a few minutes, but when he looked up, he was smiling.

Ted smiled back and the two boys went into action. Ted filled his spoon with peas and said, "Watch this!" Peas flew all over the cafeteria like green snot. *Bam. Bam. Bam.* The fourth-grade table got pelted with peas.

Dominick laughed and loaded up his spoon with mashed potatoes and green relish. "Oh, no!" Emily gasped as Dominick sent his food flying right at the fourth graders. *Splat. Splat. Splat.*

The fourth graders didn't waste any time. Peas, mashed potatoes, and pot roast flew through the air. The third graders screamed and ducked. "Food fight!" Ted yelled. He grabbed a handful of pot roast and flung it into the air.

Unfortunately, Principal Pellman walked into the cafeteria at just that moment. Ted's pot roast caught her right across the face. Everyone stopped as Principal Pellman wiped brown ooze from her eyes. She took one look at Ted and jerked her thumb toward her office.

On the way back from the cafeteria, Tommy, Frank, Ryan, and Emily all walked with Jake. Dominick walked in front of them, bopping kids on the head with his bag of carrots. "How am I ever going to get Dominick back to the swamp?" Jake asked his friends quietly.

The five friends watched Ted walk out of the principal's office and join Dominick. Ryan shook his head and said, "We have two nasty horrible creatures loose in the third grade."

"Ryan!" Emily said sharply. "You

49

shouldn't call Jake a nasty horrible creature!"

Jake held up his hand. "That's okay. We know that's what webless creatures call us, and it doesn't bother me."

"I'm not talking about you," Ryan said, pointing to the two troublemaking boys ahead of them in the hall. "I'm talking about Dominick and Ted."

Tommy laughed. "I don't think there's anything we can do about them," he said.

"Especially Ted," Emily said. "He's been a stinker since first grade."

Jake rubbed his dry webless hand against his chin. "Maybe we can do something. I have an idea."

9

A Plan

After school, the five friends met at Tommy's house while Dominick went home with Ted.

"We need to get you and Dominick back into the water," Emily told Jake. "I know you've had another carrot, but I'm still worried about you being out of the swamp for so long. Do you think it will hurt you?"

Jake shrugged his shoulders. "I don't know. This is uncharted swamp monster territory."

Ryan had to smile. "I guess you're like a swamp monster experiment."

"Nothing like this came in my Junior Science Kit," Frank told his friends.

"Tell us your idea, Jake," Emily suggested.

Tommy put some cookies on the kitchen table, and the kids helped themselves while Jake explained his plan. "We have to make being a human seem like a terrible thing," Jake said.

Frank poured himself a glass of milk. "What are you talking about?" he asked as cookie crumbs dribbled out of his mouth.

"I get it," Emily said. "If we make being a human feel like the most awful thing in the world, Dominick won't like it anymore."

"Exactly how do we do that?" Tommy asked.

Jake picked up an Oreo and bit into it. It tasted so good he could hardly think straight. Getting Dominick not to like things

52

like this would not be easy. Jake finished chewing and answered, "We could make a list of all the horrible things you can think of and then read it to Dominick."

"It's worth a try," Emily said.

"I've got a pencil," Tommy said. He wrote AWFUL THINGS at the top of a piece of white lined paper.

"Homework and tests," Ryan offered, and the kids nodded in agreement.

"Chores," Emily said.

"We need really bad stuff," Tommy said. "Like wars."

Jake shook his head. "Dominick actually likes fighting. And we have to do chores back in the swamp, too."

"My dad says taxes are the worst," Ryan suggested.

The phone rang and Tommy answered it. "Sure," he said into the phone.

After Tommy hung up, he looked at his friends and said, "We're sunk. Dominick is spending the night with Ted. We won't even see him until tomorrow."

"There's no telling what kind of trouble those two will cause tonight," Emily said. "How are we going to tell him what's on our list?"

"I don't think this list thing is going to work," Ryan told his friends. "I think we need to do something else. Something bigger."

"Like what?" Tommy asked.

"I think we need to get his carrot supply away from him," Frank said.

Emily slapped her hand on the table. "That's it!" she shouted. "But how?"

"We can just grab it," Ryan said.

"Haven't you seen how big Dominick

is?" Emily said. "And you already *know* how mean Ted is."

"Dominick can be kind of mean, too," Jake added.

"We'll have to swipe it when they aren't looking," Tommy said.

"We have to go over to Ted's house," Jake said firmly, "and we have to do it tonight."

10

Real Monsters

Squish. Squish.

Squish. Squish.

"What's that noise?" Ryan said as the four kids walked down the street toward Ted's house.

Squish. Squish. "Um," Jake said. "That's me. I think I'm changing back." He held his hands up. They were a light green and thin webs spread between his fingers.

Tommy pulled a small carrot out of his pants pocket. "Here, eat this quick. I brought it just in case."

Jake knew he had to do it, but he also knew what would happen. He took a deep breath before taking the carrot from Tommy. Then he bit into it and chewed. In just a few seconds, the entire street and the trees around him started to spin. *Bam!* Jake fell to the ground. The next thing he knew Emily had her hand on his shoulder. She was shaking him.

"Are you okay?" Emily said.

Jake smiled up into Emily's pretty brown eyes, and Emily smiled back.

Jake's stomach did a flip-flop when he looked at Emily. "I . . . I'm fine," he said, jumping up from the ground.

"Then let's get this show on the road," Frank said. Ryan, Tommy, and Frank started down the sidewalk again.

Jake rubbed his temple. Turning into a human sure did give him a headache. Emily took his hand and guided him down the street. Jake didn't pull his hand away.

In fact, he liked having Emily hold his hand. It felt strangely nice, even if her hand was very dry.

"This is Ted's house," Ryan said. "I just hope we can find those carrots."

The minute Emily pushed the doorbell, a cold blast of water soaked her face. "Ahhhh!" she screamed.

Frank, Ryan, Tommy, and Jake got blasted, too. Jake liked it, but Ryan yelled, "Stop it!"

Dominick and Ted came around the corner of the house, laughing. They each carried a huge red water gun. "Aren't these great?" Dominick said. "They almost always make people scream."

Ted snickered. "Especially when you put ice in the water."

"That's not funny," Emily snapped.

Dominick shrugged. "Sorry, we didn't mean to make you mad. Let's shake hands and make up."

Emily didn't like to hold a grudge so she held out her hand. Dominick shook her hand. Emily squealed and turned up her nose. "Ewww! What is that?" she asked, holding up her hand.

Brown gooey ooze covered her fingers. "Ooops," Dominick said. "I must have forgotten to wash after our snack." He elbowed Ted, and they both cracked up laughing.

"Ted's house is great," Dominick continued. "He has snacks everywhere. He even has a machine that shoots out fluffy white stuff you can eat."

Ted laughed again. "Yeah, we made a popcorn mountain in my basement."

Emily wasn't impressed. She just wanted to wash the sticky peanut butter off her hand.

"Wait a minute," Dominick said. "I have to show you something." Dominick and Ted raced off around the back of the house.

Emily wiped her fingers on the grass in the front yard.

"We have to get Dominick to change back," Jake told his friends. "Before he and Ted cause more trouble."

Emily agreed, "Yeah, before they smear peanut butter over the whole city."

While they were waiting in Ted's front yard, Jake saw something he couldn't believe.

Two huge ugly monsters raised their hairy claws and lumbered toward him. Blood dripped from their fangs as the monsters roared, "Get them!"

11

Swamp

Emily giggled. "They aren't real monsters," she explained. "Ted and Dominick just have on old Halloween costumes."

Of course, Ted and Dominick slapped each other on the back and laughed at Jake's reaction.

"Halloween?" Jake said, keeping an eye on Dominick and Ted in their strange get-ups. They each had ugly plastic masks over their faces and big hairy gloves on their hands. "What is this Halloween?"

"Kids dress up in strange outfits and get candy," Ryan explained.

Dominick licked his lips. "Candy is the best. Ted has a lot of candy at his house."

Jake tried to ignore the creepy evil eye on Dominick's costume. Jake saw the bag of carrots sticking halfway out of Dominick's pocket.

"Hey, Dominick, can I see your gloves?" Jake asked. "They remind me of Uncle Dave when he had that web fungus."

Jake acted like he was reaching for Dominick's funny gloves, but instead Jake grabbed the carrot bag out of Dominick's pocket and started running.

"Give me that back," Dominick screamed. Dominick and Ted ran after Jake, but Emily

and Tommy tried to stop them. Emily put out her foot and tripped Ted. Tommy grabbed Dominick and held him tight.

Dominick pushed Tommy away and the chase was on. All the kids ran after Jake. Ted struggled to his feet and caught up with Dominick. Ted and Dominick were still wearing their Halloween costumes.

Jake raced down the street toward the

swamp. "Hurry!" Emily hollered behind him. Jake ran as fast as he could, but suddenly, he slowed down. His webs were coming back and they made running in Tommy's old tennis shoes hard. Quickly, Jake reached down and snatched the shoes off. He threw them back at Dominick to slow him down.

It didn't work. Ted and Dominick were gaining on Jake. Finally, Jake arrived at the clearing by the swamp. He yelled at Dominick, "We have to go back. We belong in the swamp!"

"What are you talking about?" Ted yelled. "Nobody belongs in that mud pond."

Dominick didn't want to turn into a real monster in front of Ted. It might spoil all their fun. "Give me those carrots!" Dominick shouted and rushed at Jake, but Jake was too quick for his cousin.

"NO!" Dominick screamed as Jake threw the carrot bag into the swamp. The bag sailed high into the air before landing with a thump and a splash in the thick green water.

Dominick waded into the swamp water to get the carrots, but he wasn't fast enough. A green hand shot up out of the water and pulled the bag under.

12

Dreaming

"HA! We got you!" Jake cried. "Now you have to come back with me," he told Dominick.

Dominick shook his head. "I can get more carrots. Webless creatures have this place called a grocery store. They have more carrots than I'll ever need. If you eat some carrots, more appear there the next day. It's like a miracle."

"But you have to go back," Emily explained. "If you don't, you'll get sick and pass out. That's what happened to Jake the first time he turned into a human."

Ted had a strange look on his face. "What are you guys talking about?"

Dominick shook his head. "No, no, no. I'm not ready yet." Dominick's face turned green and his hair started looking finlike. "Give me more carrots quick. I'm already changing back."

"Maybe you could visit again sometime," Frank reassured him.

Ryan gulped and stared at Dominick's fin. "You could come over summer vacation."

Ted stared as Dominick fell onto the ground. His face and hands were still covered with the costume, but his arms and legs were turning green. "What's wrong with him?" Ted asked Jake.

Jake pulled off Dominick's mask and gloves. The huge fin on top of Dominick's head and his webbed hands popped out.

Ted backed away. "This isn't funny," he said. "I'm going to tell Mrs. Varga you guys played a mean trick on me. Dominick, say something!"

Dominick's body did his talking for him. Green scales and a long, pointed tail popped out of his clothes. Ted screamed and ran away.

Ryan, Tommy, Frank, and Emily just stared at Dominick like he was from another planet. The costume ripped to shreds as the scales popped out on Dominick's body. Dominick started to say something, but he fainted before he could get a word out.

"Thanks for all your help," Jake told his friends. "Can you help me get him into the water?" Dominick was big, so it took all five of them to pull and push him into the muddy water.

"What about you?" Emily asked Jake as they stood side by side at the edge of the swamp.

"It shouldn't be long now," Jake said. "My gills popped out an hour ago." Sure enough, before the kids' eyes, Jake turned greener and greener.

"Are you going to be okay?" Tommy asked.

Jake waved one webbed hand in the air. "I'm getting used to this changing thing. I like hanging out with you guys, but there's no place like the swamp."

Ryan gasped when a green girl-like swamp monster stood up out of the water. "I need to go home and rest," he said, rubbing his eyes.

"This is Nancy," Jake said to his human friends. "She's my sister."

Jake and Nancy took Dominick's arms

and dragged him deeper into the slimy water. Jake waved a webbed hand. "Thanks for everything," he said. The four kids watched as Jake and Nancy disappeared under the murky water with Dominick. In a few minutes, only a ripple remained where they had been.

"Good-bye!" Tommy waved.

Frank shook his head. "Did I really see that or was I dreaming?"

Emily laughed. "You were definitely dreaming."

13

Friends

But it wasn't a dream because the next day Dominick was back at the edge of the swamp. "I guess I wasn't very nice to you," he told Emily and Tommy. "Thanks for helping to get me back to the swamp."

"We're just glad you and Jake are okay," Emily said. "That's why we came back today."

Jake stood up out of the water. Swampweed dripped off his scaly green skin. "Thanks for everything," he said.

"I've learned my lesson," Dominick explained. "Besides, Jake and I are both

grounded for a whole month. We're sup-
posed to be fishing for supper right now."

Jake looked over his shoulder and nodded. "If our parents catch us this close to
dry land, we'll be shelling clams for the rest
of our lives."

Emily reached out over the swamp water
and put her hand on Jake's green arm. "It
was nice to see you again, even if Dominick did make things a little crazy," she
said. Jake felt warm in spite of the cool
morning breeze.

"Will we ever see you at school again?'
Tommy asked.

Jake shrugged, but Nancy popped up out
of the swamp and laughed. "You don't have
to worry about him," she said. "I'm the one
with the carrots." She held up the dripping
bag of carrots.

Jake slapped his webbed hand across his forehead, but Dominick yelled, "Great balls of mud!"

Emily grinned. "I never thought I'd have a swamp monster for a friend."

"You don't have a swamp monster for a friend," Dominick said with a frown.

"I don't?" Emily said.

A big grin spread over Dominick's face. "No, you have three swamp monster friends!"

"And a swamp monster never forgets a friend," Nancy said with a wink. "See you soon!"

About the Author

Debbie Dadey is the author and coauthor of more than one hundred fifteen books for kids, including The Adventures of the Bailey School Kids series and Ghostville Elementary. The idea for the Swamp Monster in Third Grade series came from a Bailey School book, *Swamp Monsters Don't Chase Wild Turkeys.*

Debbie lives in Colorado with her husband, three children, and two dogs. It's usually very dry in Colorado, so she hasn't seen any swamp monsters lately. But she's keeping an eye out for them.

Ready for more spooky fun?
Then take a sneak peek
at the new series from
Marcia Thornton Jones
and Debbie Dadey!

Ghostville Elementary®

#5 Stage Fright

Finally, at two o'clock in the afternoon, Mr. Morton cleared his throat. "Okay, class," he announced. "It's time for the play auditions."

A few kids groaned, but most kids cheered. Carla and Darla clapped their hands. Everyone put away their spelling worksheets and took out their copy of the book the class had been reading together.

"Remember, each part is important," Mr. Morton told the class. "And we will need many students to make the set and decorations for the play."

"Now, let's see who is interested in playing Travis?" Mr. Morton asked. Jeff, Andrew, and Cassidy raised their hands in the air.

Jeff looked at Andrew. "I thought you didn't like plays," Jeff said.

Andrew shrugged. "I thought I'd give it a try."

Andrew went first. Jeff had to admit that Andrew was pretty good. Cassidy went next and read her part out loud. Jeff sank down in his seat. Cassidy was really good, too.

When Mr. Morton called his name, Jeff walked slowly to the front of the room. Jeff turned his book to page six and opened his mouth. Nothing came out. Jeff stood frozen to the floor like time had stopped.

"What's wrong with Jeff?" Nina whispered to Cassidy.

Cassidy didn't say anything, either. She just pointed. When Nina saw what Cassidy was pointing at, Nina froze, too. . . .

Jeff stared at a strange figure hovering in

the back corner of the room. It was a girl dressed in a flowing white gown. Her long dark hair floated above her head as she bowed slightly at Jeff.

Of course, only Jeff, Cassidy, and Nina could see her. The rest of the class, including their teacher, didn't realize a new ghost was in their midst.

"Jeff? Jeff?" Mr. Morton asked. "Are you okay?"

Jeff's mouth moved, but no sound came out.

"Look at him," Andrew blurted. "He's got stage fright."

"It's a fright, all right," Nina murmured. "But it has nothing to do with a stage."

The new ghost slowly floated through the air, straight to the items the kids had brought back from the Blackburn Estate. Her slender pale finger ran along the chip on the small dish. Finally, the strange ghost paused in front of the fiddle and smiled. She gently plucked three strings. They played the same tune Cassidy had heard when they left the Blackburn Estate. The notes seemed to bounce off the walls as the ghost floated over to stand beside Jeff. The ghost tilted her head, closed her eyes, and began to sing.

Her voice was high and loud. A good dose of screeching was mixed in, though it sounded like it came from a different part of the room. . . .

Nina put her fingers in her ears. Cassidy covered her ears with her hands. Jeff stood at the front of the room and stared.

Of course, they were the only kids who saw or heard any of the ghostly antics.

"Don't you want to try out for the play?" Mr. Morton asked Jeff gently. "You don't have to if you don't want to. I can give the part to someone else."

That was enough to snap Jeff out of his stupor. He forgot all about ghosts and looked at his teacher. "Of course I want to try out," he said. "I'm perfect for this part."

Jeff tried to ignore the singing. . . . He concentrated on reading the lines for the play. "Arliss, you get out of that water," he began reading.

But the louder the new ghost sang, the louder Jeff had to yell out his part. Soon, he was shouting so loudly the kids in the front row had to cover their ears. Carla and Darla giggled and Andrew laughed out loud.

"Thank you, Jeff," Mr. Morton finally said. "I think you've showed the rest of the class that you can project your voice so all can hear."

Jeff hung his head and walked back to his seat.

Just then Huxley, the ghost dog, appeared in the middle of the room and lifted his nose toward the bookshelves. He let out a howl that Cassidy was sure shook the walls. It was so loud, in fact, that it broke the ghost sound barrier. Everyone in the class could hear the ghostly howl. Mr. Morton stopped dead in his tracks. Carla and Darla screamed. Andrew fell to the ground and hid under his desk.

Mr. Morton wiped at his glasses until he had two clear circles to see through. "What was that?" Mr. Morton gasped.

The room had suddenly grown quiet — very quiet. Cassidy, Nina, and Jeff looked around. That's when Jeff saw a tiny shadow huddled on the bookshelves.

"Oh, no," he muttered. "It can't be!"

Creepy, weird, wacky, and
funny things happen to
the Bailey School Kids!™
Collect and read them all!

The Adventures of
THE
BAILEY SCHOOL
KIDS®